WHEN I GROW UP

By Judy Ainsworth

Photographs by Belinda Durrie

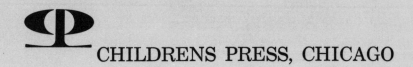

CHILDRENS PRESS, CHICAGO

For Gray and his friends who appear in this book,
and also for Sharron, Cassandra, Zoraya, and Todd

Library of Congress Catalog Card Number: 69-14686

WHEN I GROW UP

Once there was
a little boy.

He asked his mother
the same question
every morning.

"Am I a man yet,
Mommy?"

"Not yet, dear. Eat
your breakfast," his
mother would answer.

"I want to be a man,"
said the little boy.
"Why are you in
a hurry to grow up?"
asked his mother.
"Because it is fun
to be a man. When I grow
up, I can stay up late
at night."

"I can go to work."
"Good-bye, dear. See you tonight."

"When I grow up
I can work in my
office."

"I can drive a car.
I can take my children
for a ride in the country."

"When I am a man
I can be big and strong
like Daddy."

"Why can't I be a man now, Mommy?"

"Because you are not ready," said Mother.

The little boy thought about this for a while. Then he went to talk to his daddy.

"I want to be a man,"
said the little boy.
"Someday you will
be a man," said Daddy.
"But I want to be a
man now," said the boy.
"It is fun to be a man."

"It is a fine thing
to be grown up," said
Daddy. "But I remember
how much fun it was to
be a boy. Sometimes I
wish I were a boy again."

"Really?" said the boy.

"Yes," said Daddy. "I
remember how much fun it
was to run through a field.
Sometimes I found something
wonderful–

like a climbing tree,
big enough for everyone."

"I can remember spending all day building a secret hideout, when I was a boy," said Daddy.

"When you are a boy," said Daddy, "you always can play pretend games.

"You can talk about secret plans, like what you are going to do tomorrow."

"When you are a boy, tomorrow is always filled with suprises. Like finding a perfect spot to play marbles. Oh yes," said Daddy, "it is fun to be a boy."

That night when Daddy came to kiss him goodnight, the little boy said:

"Daddy, I think I will be a little boy for a few more days."

"That's fine," said Daddy. "There is plenty of time to be a man."

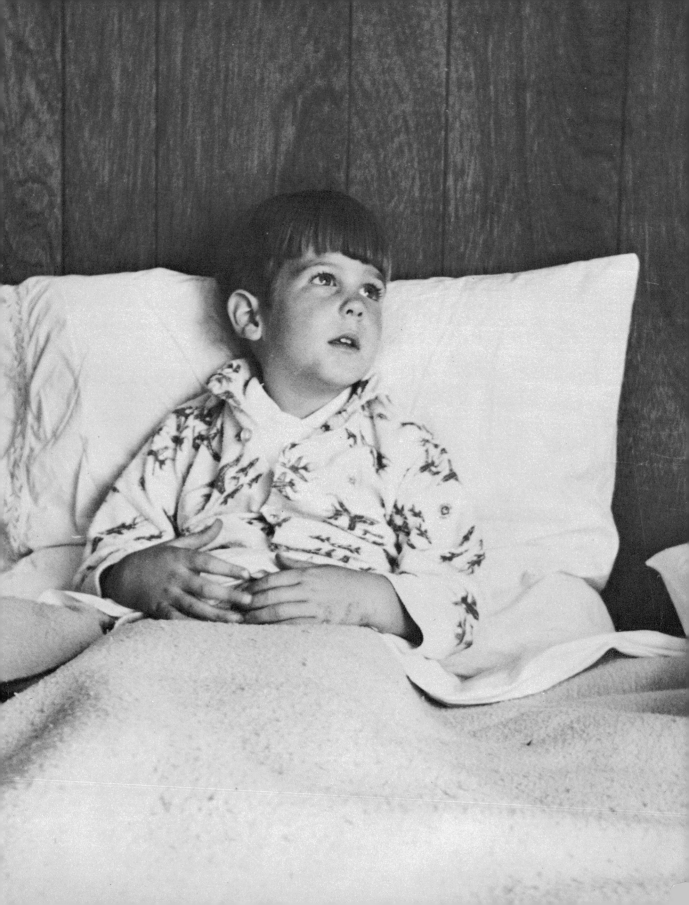